Ozzy Russell

2006

Special thanks to Claudia Cornett.

In memory of Eudena "Dee" Jenista and Helen Spagnolo Slane. *RS*

To Nicole, Evan, Hayley and Adam. You are everything to me. *SMZ*

To my mom, Jo, husband, Ash, my son, Andrew, and my girls, Ali and Christina. *KS*

To my daughter, Kat, son, Aaron, all my grandchildren, and to the memory of my mother, Aurelia Cornett. *JM*

To my girls who make me proud to be a husband and dad. *GR*

First U.S. edition 2005

Shehata, Kat.
   Come away home : hilton head is calling you home / adapted by Kat Shehata ; based on the screen story by Robert D. Slane and Stephen M. Zakman ; lyrics by Gregg Russell ; illustrations by Jo McElwee.
   p. cm.
   SUMMARY; Annie's parents force her to spend the summer in Hilton Head, South Carolina. The situation worsens when she tries to escape in her grandfather's boat.
   Audience: Ages 8-12.
   ISBN 0-9717843-3-7

   1. Summer--Juvenile fiction. 2. Hilton Head Island (S.C.)--Juvenile fiction. [1. Summer --Fiction. 2. Hilton Head Island (S.C.)-- Fiction.] I. Slane, Robert D. II. Zakman, Stephen M. III. Russell, Gregg. IV. McElwee, Jo V. Title.

PZ&.S5413Com 2005   [Fic]
                              QBI33-2039

Printed in China

Come Away Home

Hilton Head is Calling You Home

by Kat Shehata and Robert D. Slane
Illustrations by Jo McElwee
Lyrics by Gregg Russell

Angel Bea Publishing
Cincinnati, Ohio
www.angelbea.com

"It doesn't matter," I snapped at the flight attendant. Chicken or beef—what difference did it make? I wanted to be home hanging out with my friends, going shopping, that sort of thing. Instead, my parents *surprised* me with a plane ticket to Hilton Head, South Carolina.

They were forcing me to spend the summer with my grandfather, whom I barely knew. He lived in an old dumpy shack, with no cable, out in the middle of nowhere. Did I mention no cable modem? I wouldn't even be able to use my laptop to email my friends!

This trip was meant to get me out of the way so my parents could go on a second honeymoon. Alone. "Why can't I stay with my friends?" I protested. "Why do you have to dump me off at Grandpa's? I don't even know him! What am I supposed to do there?" Nothing I said mattered to Mom and Dad. They were going on their trip.

"End of discussion," Mom said. "You haven't seen Grandpa in years, Annie. It will be good for you two to get to know each other. Did I mention he has a pool and a boat?" I rolled my eyes.

When I got off the plane Grandpa was waiting for me. He had messy gray hair and was dressed in a faded tropical print shirt and baggy khaki shorts. When we got to his house, it wasn't at all what I had expected. It was much worse! There were old yellow newspapers stacked everywhere, it smelled like the backseat of a cab, and there was a record player in the corner. "Hello? Where's the CD player?"

I dropped my suitcase on the floor and looked out the window. Mom was right; he did have a pool and a boat. A dirty, green, algae-filled pool and a little boat that looked a hundred years old.

"Well, what should we do first, Annie?" Grandpa asked.

"I don't know," I mumbled, trying not to burst into tears. I couldn't believe my parents were doing this to me.

"Well, for starters you can put your things upstairs in your room," Grandpa said. "While you are doing that, I'll make us something to eat."

When I got upstairs to *my room* I saw an old-fashioned phone next to the bed. I put down my suitcase and called my best friend, Hayley. "There is no way I am staying here one day, let alone the whole summer. Get me out of here!" I begged. "Go online and find out where I can catch a bus or something. I will call you back later."

While Hayley was working on my escape route, I went downstairs to see what Grandpa was cooking up. The food on the plane was disgusting, and I was starving. On the table there were two mismatched place settings and two glasses of sweet tea. I hate sweet tea. Grandpa came out of the kitchen carrying two defrosted frozen dinners. "Chicken or beef?" he asked.

I sighed. "It doesn't matter." While we ate we talked about school, Mom and Dad, and what kids do *nowadays* as opposed to what kids did when he was little. Grandpa seemed okay. However, I wasn't about to change my mind about escaping.

After dinner, I told Grandpa I was tired and went upstairs. I called Hayley back. "Yes, there is a bus station in a town called Beaufort, but it's too far to walk. You either have to swim or get a ride," she said jokingly. I couldn't help but smile. Hayley was great. She had found out where the bus station was, what time I needed to get there, and how much a ticket cost.

I had about a hundred bucks worth of saved allowance with me, which was just enough for a ticket to New York and a decent meal. The only problem was how was I going to get to the bus station. I looked out the window. My eyes followed the path down to the dock. There it was like a knight in shining armor…Grandpa's old boat.

Before I went to bed that night I set the alarm on my text messenger. When the alarm buzzed at 4:30 a.m., I was ready to go. I had my suitcase and money for my ticket. I just had to get that old boat started and headed toward Beaufort. I crawled out the window onto the roof and tossed my suitcase to the ground. Then I jumped and landed softly on the sand.

Down at the dock I untied the boat, tossed my suitcase aboard, and stepped in. I pulled the cord on the engine and it made a loud rumble. It didn't start though. I pulled it again and again until the engine stayed on. I worried all the noise had woken Grandpa up. I didn't look back to see if he was there. I stared straight ahead and steered the boat the best I could.

After a mile or so I spotted the Hilton Head Bridge. I recognized it since we crossed it on the way home from the airport. Hayley said Beaufort was just north of Hilton Head so I knew I was going the right way.

Suddenly the engine started to sputter. I groaned. Maybe the boat was out of gas. I tried to start the engine again and it gave a couple of loud burps. Then it just died. With no power from the engine, the boat drifted. I couldn't make it go the way I wanted. I was stuck in open water. I stood up and pulled again on the cord thinking maybe it had just stalled like our old lawn mower used to do. I pulled and pulled and then *SPLASH!* I lost my balance and fell in the water.

My jeans and tennis shoes were pulling me down into the salt water. "Help!" I screamed. "Someone help me!" I was trying to keep my head up as the boat drifted further and further away. I screamed for my mom and dad. I even yelled for Grandpa. I was getting tired trying to keep my head above water. Waves slapped at my face and suddenly I was under the surface looking up at the bottom of the boat. I thought I heard a dog barking. That was the last thing I remembered.

When I woke up, I didn't know where I was. I was lying on a sofa in a fancy house with a window that looked out to the ocean. Where in the world was I? And why was I wearing some other girl's clothes? I sat up, coughing, and then jumped when a big sloppy dog rushed toward me wagging his tail. "You are lucky he heard you yelling for help," a woman said as she entered the room.

"Where am I? Who are you? Why am I wearing these clothes?" I asked. "You are safe here," she answered. "My name is Sonya. This is my house. And I put those clothes on you so you wouldn't freeze to death. Do you remember anything about the accident?"

Just then I heard a knock on the door. "Come on in, Gregg," Sonya said. "This is the man who saved your life." The man opened the door and stepped inside. He looked like a *mountain man* because he had a wild beard and long hair. "I got my keys," the man said to Sonya. "Is she all right, or should we take her to the hospital?"

"I'm fine, I promise. I have to get back to my grandfather's house," were the first words I said to him.

"You are lucky to be alive," he replied. He was right. I felt so stupid. I hoped Grandpa wasn't getting blamed for all this. "I'm sure your grandfather must be worried sick," Gregg said. "What is his phone number?" I didn't know Grandpa's number or his address. "Well, then I will take you to the sheriff's station. I'm sure he can help."

Sonya went to the kitchen to bring out some snacks. I think the smell of whatever she was cooking had woken me up from my nap. "Thanks for saving me," I said. "My name is Annie. What's your name?"

"Gregg," he replied. His face was so serious like I was questioning him.
"I know these aren't Sonya's clothes. Are they yours?" I asked jokingly.
"No, they were my daughter's," he said with the same stern look. "Let's get you to the police station."

Sonya came out of the kitchen carrying a tray of stuff I had never tasted before: home-made pimento cheese sandwiches, hush puppies, and crab cakes. "All right, y'all. No one's going anywhere until we eat up these snacks," she said.

After we ate our snacks, we got in Gregg's truck and headed for the station. It was a very quiet ride, so I tried to make conversation. "So, where's your daughter?" I asked.

Gregg kept his eyes on the road and replied, "She died."
"Oh, I'm sorry to hear that. What happened?" I asked.
"My daughter and my wife were killed in a car crash," he answered.

His eyes were getting watery so I tried to change the subject. "Do you know what happened to my grandfather's boat?" I asked.

"No," he said. "I was too busy saving you to worry about that old boat."
"Oh, yeah," I said. "Well, if you see it will you let me know?"

When we got to the police station Grandpa was standing outside talking to the sheriff. When Grandpa saw me in Gregg's truck he put his hand on his chest as a sign of relief. I felt so bad for losing his boat and scaring him like I did. When Gregg parked the truck I didn't want to get out.

I watched as Gregg walked over to Grandpa and the sheriff. I could tell by his hand gestures and facial expressions that he was telling them what happened to me and Grandpa's boat. A few minutes later I got in the car with Grandpa. We didn't speak the whole way home. He didn't ask, "Why did you try to run away?" or "Where's my boat?" and I didn't say anything either like, "Did you call my parents?" or "Am I grounded for the rest of the summer?"

When we got home I went straight to my room and took a nap. I was still exhausted from the whole ordeal. I woke up several hours later and felt a little better. I went downstairs to face my grandpa.

"Are you hungry, Annie?" Grandpa asked. After what I had done I couldn't believe he was being so nice to me. I felt bad all over again.

"Yes, I'm starving," I said. "Do you have any pizza or chips?" I was happy to see Grandpa crack a little smile and actually make eye contact with me.

"No," he said chuckling. "Chicken or beef?" Seriously, all Grandpa had in his fridge were frozen dinners, ketchup, and homemade sweet tea.

"If you're not going to lock me in my room for the rest of the summer, can we go shopping?" I asked. "No offense, but we need to stock up on some *real* food." I grinned to soften my words. "Oh, and by the way, all my stuff was in my suitcase, which is missing in action with your boat."

Grandpa said we were going to *The Pig*. On the way there, we stopped to buy some clothes at a few of the local shops. All their shirts and shorts were "islandy." Everything had palmetto trees, sunsets, beach scenes, and this candy-cane-colored lighthouse.

I knew my friends would crack up if they saw me dressed in this stuff. I didn't mind, though. It was a lot of fun trying everything on and "modeling" for Grandpa. He was having as much fun as I was! "Look at you, Annie. You look just like your mom when she was a girl," he laughed. "Yuck," I thought.

The next stop was a grocery store that the locals call *The Pig*. Grandpa pushed the cart while I loaded it with fresh veggies, fruits, yogurt, hot dogs, pizza fixings, and of course the 3 C's: chips, chocolate, and cola. "Don't even look at the frozen food aisle!" I warned Grandpa. He laughed.

On the way home, we stopped at a roadside fresh seafood stand. Grandpa got some shrimp for dinner while I picked out some peaches. On the way back to the car I had to ask Grandpa, "Did you call Mom and Dad?"

"No. I didn't get a chance yet," he replied. "Do you want me to? They will probably want to lock you in your room for the rest of the summer."

"Very funny. Although you may be right," I said. "I am so sorry I lost your boat."

Grandpa looked at me and said, "When you were gone I wasn't worried about losing my boat."

I felt bad for acting so selfish. What was I thinking? I really wanted to get Grandpa's boat back. "Do you know where the man who saved me lives?" I asked. "I need to return his daughter's clothes."

When Grandpa and I got home I told him to relax while I cooked dinner. I could tell Grandpa was looking forward to it because he licked his lips and rubbed his hands together. He's so funny.

In the kitchen, there wasn't much to work with. I made do with what he had and got busy chopping, peeling, and slicing. I had found an old recipe for seafood gumbo in a drawer that must have been my grandma's. She died many years ago. I had never made a recipe with fresh seafood before. I was glad I had my grandma's instructions.

While the gumbo was simmering, I looked in on Grandpa. He was sitting at the table with my headphones on! He was bobbing his head and making funny faces as he listened to my CD!

After dinner, Grandpa dusted off his old record player and put on some of *his* music. He started humming along with Tommy Dorsey and tapping his feet in time with the music. Then *whoosh!* He grabbed me and twirled me around. I was laughing so hard I could barely keep my balance. It was funny to see Grandpa acting so silly.

"This dance is called the Jitterbug," he said almost out of breath.

Later that night we had peach cobbler for dessert outside on the porch. We were being eaten alive by tiny mosquitoes so Grandpa went in to get a citronella candle and some bug repellant. When he came back he brought out his old chess set. I had never played before. "You are going to be a master at this game before the summer is over," Grandpa said.

Before I went to bed I called Hayley to tell her what happened. "Well, at least you're okay," she said.

"Better than okay," I corrected. "I am having a blast with Grandpa!"

Early the next morning I rode Grandpa's old bike over to Gregg's house to return his daughter's clothes. He lived just down the beach from Grandpa's house. Grandpa told me Gregg used to be a pretty well-known singer on the island. He was surprised to see him looking so *rugged*. Grandpa said that after Gregg lost his wife and daughter, he stopped performing.

I walked to the back of Gregg's house and he looked surprised to see me. "I just wanted to give back your daughter's things," I explained.

"I'm glad you're here," he said. "I have a surprise for you." I couldn't believe my eyes. It was Grandpa's boat!

The boat was in bad shape. It wasn't much worse than it was before, but the engine needed a lot of work and the boat desperately needed a fresh coat of paint. "Gregg, do you know anything about fixing boats?" I asked.

For the first time, I saw Gregg's smile. "Do you want to help me fix it up?" he asked.

"Sure!" I said eagerly. "What do we need to do?" It turned out Gregg knew a lot about boat engines. I sanded off the old paint while Gregg worked on the engine. Sonya saw us working and came over to help, too.

"Grandpa says Gregg is a singer," I said to Sonya. Sonya looked over at Gregg, who was out of earshot. "Well, he *used* to be one," she answered. "He put his guitar away after he lost his family. I guess he doesn't feel like singing anymore."

I felt sad for Gregg. It was so nice of him to help me. I wished there was something I could do for him before the summer was over.

After we worked all day, I made it back to Grandpa's house just in time for dinner. "Where have you been, Annie? I almost called the sheriff again," Grandpa said.

"I have been very busy working on something," I replied. "It's a surprise, so no more questions, okay?"

After dinner Grandpa pulled an old photo album out of a box. There were pictures of Mom when she was little, Grandma and Grandpa, and even a picture of Gregg!

"That picture was taken at Harbour Town," Grandpa explained. "Gregg used to sing there in front of that tree. It's called the Liberty Oak. There's a festival there in a few weeks. We can go if you like."

"I would love to go!" I said. While Grandpa was looking for more pictures, he found an old record album. He handed it to me. "Oh my goodness!" I said. "Is that Gregg?"

The next day I got up super early and hustled to Gregg's house. "How long is it going to take to fix Grandpa's boat?" I yelled as I pedaled towards him. "There's something else I want to do before the summer is over. Do you still have your guitar? Will you sing that song about Harbour Town?" I asked.

Gregg looked completely stumped as I sang the chorus: *I love this Harbour and it means so much to me.*

"Grandpa has one of your albums," I explained. "You know, you might be good enough to sing at the festival in Harbour Town."

Gregg's bushy beard shook as he chuckled. "Well," he said, "let's work on the boat first. Then, I will *think* about Harbour Town."

Over the next few weeks I worked with Gregg and Sonya fixing up the boat. Grandpa and I spent time playing chess, dancing to *our* music, sharing stories, and doing *touristy* stuff like miniature golf and shopping at the outlet malls.

The summer went by so quickly. Of course I missed my mom and dad and my friends, and I was looking forward to seeing them. On the other hand, I felt like I had just gotten to know Grandpa and I knew I would miss him, too. The night before my flight back home, Grandpa and I had one more special night planned—the festival in Harbour Town.

I couldn't wait to get to the festival! I kept thinking about Gregg. I hoped everything was going to work out for him. I was leaving to go back home to New York in the morning, so if I didn't see him at the festival, I might never see him again. When we got to Harbour Town, there was so much to do. There were food booths, local artists displaying their work, and people twisting balloons into animal-shaped hats. It was hard to decide what to do first!

"Oh, look. There's the red and white lighthouse that's on my shirt," I said to Grandpa.

"Yep, it's called the Harbour Town Lighthouse," he replied.

I heard music and turned my attention toward the Liberty Oak. A huge crowd was forming around the small stage in front of the tree. Grandpa and I followed our ears and became part of the crowd. "What are they trying to see?" I wondered. Just then a familiar voice floated over to us. It was Gregg! He was singing the song on his album:

I love this Harbour and it means so much to me…

"Way to go, Gregg!" I said to Grandpa. We made our way through the crowd to get a better look. I saw Sonya just ahead at the foot of the stage. Gregg saw me with Grandpa and nodded when we made eye contact. When he finished singing everybody cheered. The audience wanted more! Gregg strummed his guitar and announced, "This next song is dedicated to my new friend, Annie." Grandpa hugged me proudly. Everyone sang along with Gregg as he performed his Hilton Head song:

Come away, come away home with me…

Grandpa and I stayed at the festival until very late that night. The next morning it was time for me to go back home to New York. I hugged Grandpa good-bye and told him there was a *surprise* for him in the garage. "Don't look until I'm gone," I ordered.

Grandpa had a gift for me, too. He handed me a package wrapped in newspaper. "Well, then you can't open yours till you get home either," he teased. I wish I could have seen the look on Grandpa's face when he saw his newly remodeled boat in the garage.

When I got on the plane, I unwrapped the package and found Grandpa's chess set with a note. "*Practice up. But don't get too good. Love, Grandpa.*" All the way home I held my chess set and thought about Grandpa and our special summer together in Hilton Head. I hummed the words to our song that meant so much to me:

Come away, come away home with me…

Come Away Home
by Gregg Russell

Come away, come away home with me.
Where the sun meets the sea,
Soft ocean breezes sing through the trees.
Come away, come away home with me.
Where the wind whispers that,
Children can be what they wanna be.
Come away home, Hilton Head's calling you home.
Harbour Town's waiting, come home.
Dolphins are playing, come home.
Sea gulls are saying come home.
Come home, come away home.
Come away, come away home with me.
When the light shines from the lighthouse,
It beckons me to the sea.
Oh, Carolina, there's nothing much finer,
Than you gently calling to me.

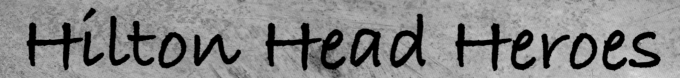

Hilton Head Heroes

The goal of Hilton Head Heroes is to help seriously ill children and their families "create memories that will last a lifetime."

When a child is seriously ill, the entire family is affected emotionally and financially. Hilton Head Heroes is dedicated to bringing children suffering from life-threatening illnesses and their families to Hilton Head Island, South Carolina, for a cost-free resort vacation.

While on vacation, families enjoy deluxe accommodations at private homes or villas and receive gift certificates to Hilton Head Island's favorite restaurants. They can also choose to go on a dolphin cruise, play miniature golf, kayak, ride bikes through the island's oak-lined trails, or just relax on the beach and build sand castles.

For most of the families it is the first time since their child has been diagnosed with an illness that they can be together as a family, away from the daily intervention of hospitals and medical treatment.

Hilton Head Heroes is a nonprofit organization. They make these dream vacations a reality with help from dedicated volunteers and generous support from vendors and the community.

For more information about Hilton Head Heroes visit their website www.hiltonheadheroes.org.

Hilton Head Heroes is a full 501C3 organization.